Ned Visits New York

BY KIP COSSON

First Edition 2006

Third Printing 2009

Published by Kip Kids of New York
KipKids@aol.com

For information address: Kip Kids of New York, 85 Christopher Street, Suite #5B, New York, NY   10014

Text and Illustrations © 2006
by Kipton P. Cosson

Visit Us At www.KipKids.com

ISBN 978-0-9789384-0-6

Printed in the United States of America

Artist and Author: Kipton P. Cosson

I honor my Mom & Dad with this book.

For Kamie, Ben, Spencer & Jake

Acknowledgments:

I would like to thank my friends and family for their support and help with this book. For without them this book would not have turned out the way it did. I owe the following a big thank you:

Cat　Jenny & Alan　Bruce　Avelene　Dottie　Dick　Don　Sanja　Aim　Bobby　Cindy　Terry

A big, warm Texas thank you to my best friend Jene, who has challenged me to go even further with this book than I thought I could, but also helped me to know when to stop. Her help and support have meant the world to me.

I dedicate my book to John who encouraged me to do this book. He was there for me with his support and feedback through the whole process with this book. A big Norwegian "Tusen Takk" (thanks) to him.

A big Peanut Butter & Jelly thank you to Alanna Pass for allowing me to use her Peanut Butter & Jelly design in my book.

A big cheese thank you to Rob Kaufelt at Murray's Cheese.

Ned Penguin of the South Pole was feeling crowded and stressed. He said to himself, "I need a rest!"

Ned was not sure where to go for a vacation.
So he placed a note in a bottle and tossed it in the sea.
Wherever it landed would be the place he would go and see.

Along with three playful dolphins the bottle drifted North
as the gigantic ocean rocked them back and forth.

Soon the bottle floated into New York harbor
and was discovered by a mouse...
A tiny little mouse named Meece.

Ned and Meece became pen pals through snail mail.
They had a lot in common as they wrote back and forth.
They both liked to fish and each could wiggle his tail.

One day a postcard arrived!
What happiness Ned felt as he twirled his tail piece.
He had an invitation to visit his new friend Meece.

Off to New York Ned went on a whim and a whale.
Friends waved good-bye and wished him well.

As Ned crossed the equator,
he saw a gator towing a freighter.
Oh, how hot the sizzling sun felt!
He quickly opened his umbrella so his iceberg would not melt.

Ned was on very thin ice as he entered the bay.
A very tall, green lady pointed the way.
With Meece in sight, Ned knew he had arrived-
N E W   Y O R K   C I T Y !

The next few days were so much fun-
So many things to see and do,
Ned was one happy penguin!

CONEY ISLAND

On Ned's first day they walked and they gawked,
and they gawked and they walked.
When they looked up to the sky, the buildings were so tall,
Ned and Meece felt very small.

Ned felt at home in Central Park.
He LOVED to skate.
Back home he was the king of figure eights.
Meece, on the other hand, jiggled like jelly
and looked so silly.

The third day, they zipped to the zoo.
Meece saw a snake and didn't know what to do.
He cried out in fear, "Let's get out of here!"
It began to rain so away they raced to catch a train.

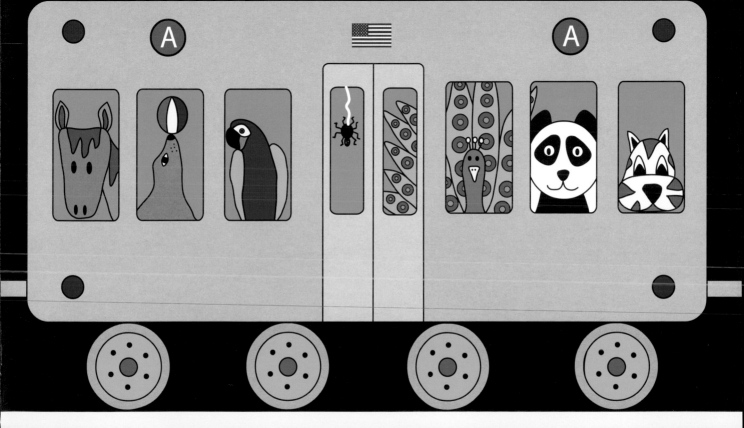

Oh, how fast it moved through the tunnel.

Title: The Cheese Dance

At the art museum
Ned's belly began to rumble and tumble.
They dashed to Greenwich Village
to quiet the grumble.

THIS IS *Murray's* CHEESE

OPEN

**They dined at Meece's favorite place
and munched on feta, cheddar, and mozzarella.
Afterwards they paid their tab,
and grabbed a cab.**

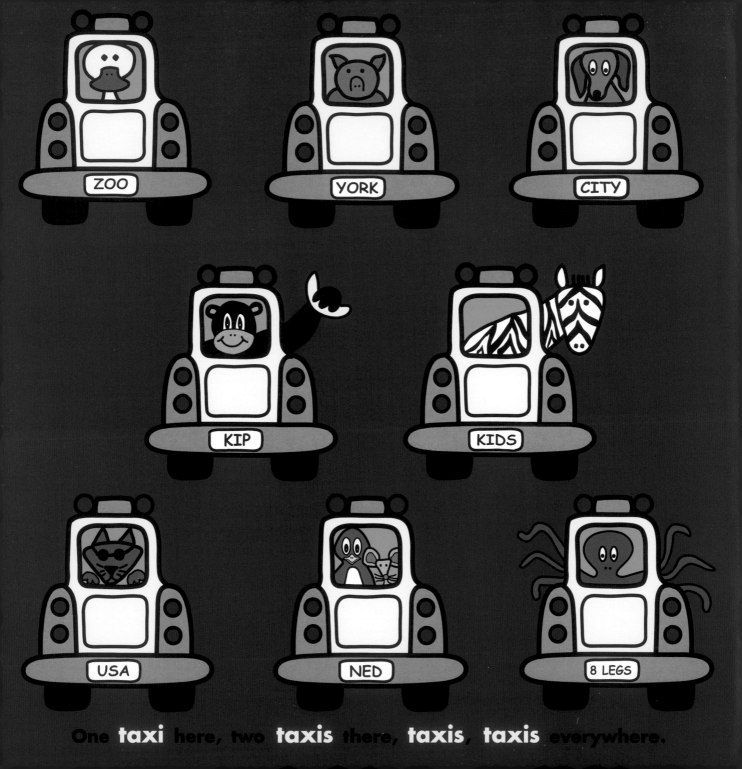

One taxi here, two taxis there, taxis, taxis everywhere.

Yellow here, **yellow** there, **yellow, yellow** everywhere.

DO NOT TOUCH

On their fourth day of sightseeing,
Ned and *Meece* saw something very old and very tall
at the museum in the great big hall.

Next, they tottered and toddled
along Fifth Avenue.
All of a sudden something icky and sticky
fell from the sky.
It splattered Ned's head
and almost got Meece in the eye!

Fire Truck

KEEP BACK
200 FEET

Dinosaur

Dump Truck

Cheese

Heart

Best Friends

Moon & Stars

Piggy

On day five they strolled along a crowded street fair,
and saw a rainbow of tee shirts hanging in the air.
They met the very cool artist selling his shirts to wear.

They took the subway to Brooklyn and rode in the last car.
As the train moved above ground,
They looked from the window and saw all around.

Ned waddled as he walked.
Meece squeaked as he talked.
So they waddled and they walked;
they squeaked and they talked
across the Brooklyn Bridge.

Starring
Peanut Butter

PB

And Jelly

THE BIG APPLE

The Monster

MY ABC

Who Loved
To Read

Give
Peas
A Chance

ROCKET
TO THE
MOON

Best Musical

OPENING NIGHT!!

SOLD OUT

BRILLIANT

42nd

NYC

The sixth day they rode through Times Square
to catch a Broadway show...

B R O A D W A Y...
Curtain up, lights down,
singing and dancing all around.
Ned was wide-eyed and completely spellbound.

On Ned's last day, they saw zillions of buildings that touched the sky.
They looked like big concrete monsters way up high.
Ned hoped he might see an igloo or two,
but he did not see one from his bird's-eye view.

The week was over in a wink of an eye.
With big bear hugs they said good-bye.
Soon Ned would splash his way back home,
returning to his icy igloo dome.

Feeling rested and well,
Ned headed back south with a great story to tell.
He hopes Meece will visit very soon.

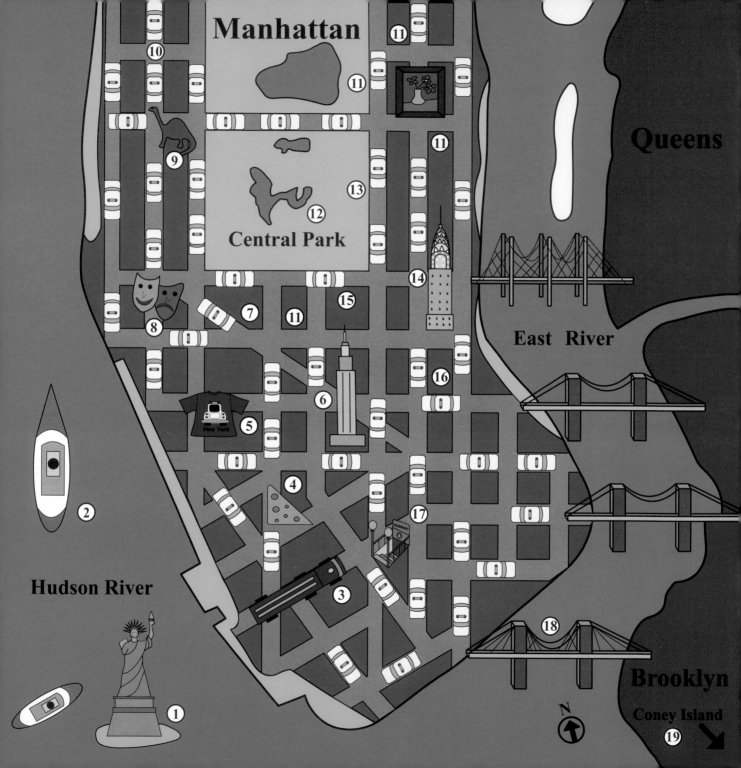

Ned's New York Check List

Place a check in each box next to each thing you have done in New York.

- ☐ **(1)** Viewed the Statue of Liberty
- ☐ **(2)** Saw a ship in New York Harbor
- ☐ **(3)** Watched a New York fire truck speed along the street
- ☐ **(4)** Ate cheese at Murray's Cheese
- ☐ **(5)** Bought a New York tee shirt from a local artist
- ☐ **(6)** Went to the top of the Empire State Building
- ☐ **(7)** Looked at the bright lights of Times Square
- ☐ **(8)** Watched a Broadway Show
- ☐ **(9)** Saw a dinosaur at the museum
- ☐ **(10)** Counted five taxi cabs in a row
- ☐ **(11)** Viewed art at one of the many museums
- ☐ **(12)** Skated in Central Park
- ☐ **(13)** Went to the zoo in Central Park
- ☐ **(14)** Saw the Chrysler Building
- ☐ **(15)** Looked at lots of tall buildings
- ☐ **(16)** Took a taxi cab ride
- ☐ **(17)** Rode the last car on the subway
- ☐ **(18)** Walked across the Brooklyn Bridge
- ☐ **(19)** Went to Coney Island and rode the roller coaster

Dinosaur

New York

New York

Fire Truck

KEEP BACK 200 FEET

Train

Train

New York

New York

About The Author/Artist

Kip Cosson is a Texan who lives in New York's Greenwich Village. He began his business in 1991 by hand painting his artwork on children's clothing. His designs have appeared in *Glamour Magazine*, *Child Magazine*, *Kids Fashion Magazine* and on the cover of *TV Guide.*

This is Kip's first children's book. If you would like to contact Kip or need more information, he can be reached at KipKids@aol.com.

Coming Fall 2009, Kip's second book, *NED & MEECE: THE WHEELS OF NEW YORK*

Visit Kip's website at www.KipKids.com